FUNNYBONES

Give the Dog a Bone

ALLAN AHLBERG · ANDRÉ AMSTUTZ

PUFFIN

On a dark dark hill
in a dark dark garden
there is a little bony dog . . .

without a bone.

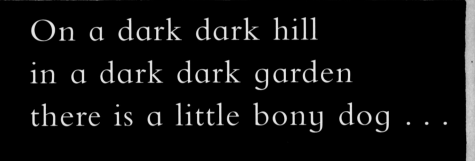

This little dog,
all alone,
sits in his kennel
and dreams of a bone.

One night, the dog skeleton goes for a walk all by himself in the dark dark street. Suddenly, he sees an old friend – and chases her.

This little dog chases a cat, hits a tree and falls down flat.

The dog skeleton
loses a bit of himself
but keeps walking.
He comes to the dark dark park
and swings on the swings
and slides on the slide.

The dog skeleton
hops out of the dark dark park,
down the dark dark street
and into the dark dark pet shop.

Suddenly, he sees some more old friends . . .

and they chase *him*.

This little dog
slips and slides.
Can anyone here
see where he hides?

Off goes the dog,
away from the pet shop,
away from the pets
and away from himself.
(He's lost another bit!)

The dog skeleton
hops up the street
and over the hill
and down the street
and round the corner.

Suddenly, he meets *another* old friend . . . and *plays* with him.

This little dog
chases a friend,
loses his tail –
is this the end?

FOG!

Bits of him gone.
Lost in the fog.
Can anyone see
what's left of the dog?

No, they can't.
The big skeleton
on his bike can't,
and the little *skeleton*
on his bike can't.
Look out!

This little dog
howls and groans.
There he is now,
just a pile of bones.

But not for long.
Soon the big skeleton
and the little skeleton
gather him up.

They follow the trail
of his lost bones,
along the street,
into the pet shop,
into the park . . .
and back home.

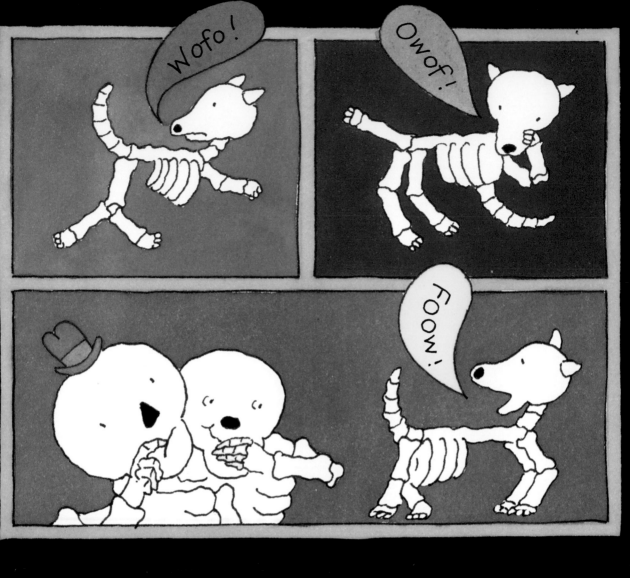

Then they put him together again.
"His legs are on wrong," says Little.
"Wofo!" barks the dog.
"His tail is on wrong," says Big.
"Owof!" barks the dog.
"His head is on wrong," say Little *and* Big.
"Foow!" barks the dog.

At last the dog skeleton
is himself again.
"Woof-woof!" he barks,
and trots off on *four* legs
to his kennel.

On a dark dark hill
in a dark dark garden
there is a little bony dog . . .

The End

PUFFIN BOOKS

UK | USA | Canada | Ireland | Australia
India | New Zealand | South Africa

Puffin Books is part of the Penguin Random House group of companies
whose addresses can be found at global.penguinrandomhouse.com.

www.penguin.co.uk   www.puffin.co.uk   www.ladybird.co.uk

First published by William Heinemann Ltd 1993
First published in Puffin Books 2005
This edition published 2018

001

Printed in China
A CIP catalogue record for this book is available from the British Library

ISBN: 978–0–241–37765–9

All correspondence to:
Puffin Books, Penguin Random House Children's
80 Strand, London WC2R 0RL